READY. SET. RESPAWN!

Published in the United States by Random House Children's Books, a division of Penguin Random House LLC, 1745 Broadway, New York, NY 10019, and in Canada by Penguin Random House Canada Limited, Toronto. Random House and the colophon are registered trademarks of Penguin Random House LLC.

rhcbooks.com
minecraft.net

Library of Congress Cataloging-in-Publication Data is available upon request.
ISBN 978-0-593-80745-3 (trade)—ISBN 978-0-593-80746-0 (lib. bdg.)—
ISBN 978-0-593-80747-7 (ebook)

Cover design by Diane Choi

Printed in the United States of America

1st Printing

READY. SET. RESPAWN!

By Caleb Zane Huett

Illustrated by Alan Batson and Chris Hill

Random House 🏠 New York

MORGAN

ASH

HARPER

PO

JODI

THEO

Prologue

A small avatar, a young boy, wandered between the giant trees of the taiga. (They looked even bigger to him because he'd never seen a tree before.) He stayed away from caves (too dark). And he was still trying to figure out water: It looked like a block, but he couldn't walk on it. And none of the fish wanted to talk to him.

The boy's favorite was mossy cobblestones because they made him wonder if there had been people here before. He hadn't picked any cobblestones up yet because he hadn't picked *anything* up. He didn't know that he could.

Every day this very unusual player did two things: **he explored, and he practiced talking.** He knew the words for most of the objects he saw. He knew numbers, too. He even knew some things he didn't fully understand, like that he was waiting for his friends to return. He knew those friends were called Morgan and Jodi, among other things.

(He spent a lot of time looking for more Morgans or Jodis in his world, but there seemed to only be one of each.)

Today, he finally heard someone new! A rattle behind a spruce tree pulled him away from inspecting mushrooms, and he ran as fast as he could to see who was visiting his home.

"HELLO!" he called. **"ARE YOU A THEO? OR A HARPER?"**

The visitor did look a little bit like a Theo. It had two legs and two arms. It had a head. The boy realized he had all those things, too!

"Are you like me?" he asked. The visitor only rattled in response. It lifted a curved stick. "That's nice," the boy said. **"I LIKE YOUR STICK."**

The visitor showed him another stick with a sharp point on the end. It brought the two sticks together.

"WOW, YOU HAVE TWO STICKS? I do not even have one." The boy smiled as the visitor pulled the second stick backward, stretching a string tied to the first stick.

"Oh, I know what that is!" the boy said, excited. "That is a *bow*!"

The visitor rattled.

"CONGRATULATIONS ON HAVING A BOW!"

The string pulled back all the way.

"Would you like to—"

Thwip.

"Ow!—be my—"

Thunk.

"OW!—FRIEND?"

Chapter 1

IRONSWORD ACADEMY IS TOTALLY SIEGE-PROOF. PLEASE LEAVE YOUR TROJAN HORSES AT HOME!

Ironsword **Academy was much, much bigger** than Morgan Mercado had expected. Tall walls surrounded an even taller building, and every gray brick shone so brightly in the sun it was hard to look at it directly.

"**More like a castle than a school,**" said Jodi, Morgan's little sister. She looked as nervous as Morgan felt. "You said it would be smaller!"

"It looked smaller on the website." He squinted up at the highest level and saw a flock of crows staring down from the roof with a hungry glint in their eyes. "**And less creepy.**"

Morgan and Jodi's school, Woodsword Middle

School, had been damaged by a huge storm a few days ago. Both it and the Stonesword Library across the street were being rebuilt and repaired. But until that was done, several students had been sent here, to **Ironsword Academy.**

"What if nobody else is actually here?" Jodi asked. "What if everybody else went to the best school ever, and we got sent to a monster school that's going to eat us? **What if they don't have art class?!**"

"You make 'no art class' sound worse than getting eaten."

"*It is worse!*" Jodi sulked.

"**Don't worry. Our friends will be here,**" said Morgan. "First days at new schools are always tough. But we're a team, and we'll stay a team no matter what."

"Thanks, Morgan. Let's go."

A teacher ushered the siblings through Ironsword's stone gate. They followed the crowd past the yard into the main building, where a group of students in sashes labeled with the Ironsword crest were giving directions.

A boy with round glasses gave them directions to room 1201, their new homeroom. It was four hallways down, then two right turns, up a staircase, down another, past the door you can hear loud jazz

music behind that you should NOT open, through a door leading outside, around the statue in the courtyard that has spooky eyes that follow you no matter where you go, through a door leading back inside, past the art room (Jodi let out a sigh of relief), up ANOTHER staircase, and then all the way at the end of that hall.

They couldn't believe it was so complicated! To help remember the directions, Morgan imagined the school was like the old castle he'd made with the rest of the Minecraft team. Having six minds all adding to one building meant it got complicated fast! Imagining Ironsword as a Minecraft build helped, but it also made him feel a little sad: their castle, like all their other builds, was gone because everything had been rebooted.

Before the storm damaged their old school, Morgan and his friends had been playing a game of Minecraft unlike any other. Their science teacher Doc Culpepper's experimental VR goggles had combined with the school's server in some sort of strange science (or alchemy) to create a very . . . *different* Minecraft experience. **The biggest difference of all was the Evoker King, an artificial intelligence who'd taken over the server.**

When the friends stopped his plan to conquer Minecraft, the Evoker King had seen the error of his ways—but had broken apart in the process. They spent what seemed like *ages* finding all the pieces and putting him back together.

"Do you think that new kid is okay?" Jodi asked as if reading Morgan's mind. She meant the strange new player the Evoker King had become when they put him back together. They'd met him once, before the school server got shut down.

"I'm sure he's fine. We told him to be careful."

"I don't think he knows what *careful* means."

Morgan nodded. But they were kids, and as

much as they would like to, they couldn't spend every minute logged into Minecraft—especially with a new school to attend.

They finally made it to room 1201, right as the bell rang. Morgan pushed the door open . . . and came face to face with his favorite teacher!

"Morgan! Jodi!" **Ms. Minerva smiled at them.** "We were afraid you wouldn't make it."

Jodi gasped. "You're our homeroom teacher *here*, too?!" Ms. Minerva was the best—not only was she an amazing teacher, but she also loved Minecraft and had helped the team many times.

"I am. You didn't think I would be building the new school *myself*, did you?" She paused. "Doc *did* want to build it herself, of course, but I convinced her to leave it to the professionals."

"AHEM!" A roomful of students all pretended to clear their throats at once. Morgan and Jodi turned to look, **and their jaws dropped in surprise.**

Everyone in their homeroom was from Woodsword. Morgan recognized students from

student council, theater club, the basketball team—**and three people he was so, so excited to see.**

"What took you so long?" Harper Houston asked.

"That's my fault," Po Chen admitted. "I told the student council to make them go the long way."

"He thought it would be fun to surprise you," Harper explained. "I hope you weren't too nervous."

Po gestured to his wheelchair. "If you go around the side of the building, there's a ramp right there." He grinned. "Sorry."

"I don't care!" Jodi exclaimed. "I'm so glad to see you I could cry!" She jumped up and down.

"And I," Theo Grayson declared, striking a dramatic pose by the window, "am here, too."

Morgan was relieved everyone was here! Well, almost everyone. He thought about Ash Kapoor, the last member of their Minecraft team, who went to another school entirely. And that new player was still in their Minecraft world somewhere.

As if reading his mind, Ms. Minerva handed him a piece of paper. "Doc asked me to make sure

you kids had these directions to the computer lab. We need to get started with school for the day, but if you're available after school, she'd like to see you."

"Of course we're available!" said Morgan, grinning at his friends.

As everyone took their seats and Ms. Minerva started explaining how things worked at their new school, Morgan couldn't stop checking and rechecking the directions on the paper. Maybe they *could* visit Minecraft here. Maybe this place wouldn't be so bad.

"I couldn't think of anything to say before," Theo whispered. **"But I am excited to see you both!"**

Morgan and Jodi turned and started to answer.

"Ahem!" Now it was Ms. Minerva's turn to fake clearing her throat. "You'll have plenty of time to talk after class, kids."

Chapter 2

THIS COMPUTER LAB ISN'T BIG ENOUGH FOR THE TWO OF US (AND ALL OF OUR COMPUTERS, AND A PILE OF EXPERIMENTAL TECHNOLOGY).

After school, everybody rushed to the new computer lab. They were eager to see Doc and maybe play some Minecraft. The lab was just a short walk away, connected to the library. Harper was the first to arrive. She waited outside for everybody else.

"This is *unacceptable*!" A man's voice boomed from behind the door. Harper jumped. Theo turned the corner just in time to hear it, and his eyes widened in surprise.

"It's *inconceivable*!" the man continued. "It's *against the rules*, it's *irregular*, and it's absolutely *not correct*!"

"Who is that?" Harper whispered. Theo peeked through the door's window to see inside.

"It's Principal Ferris," Theo explained. The man was standing in front of Doc Culpepper, his face red. He was much taller than Doc and wore a suit with a dark tie that looked as sharp as a blade. "I saw his picture on the website."

"I welcomed you and your students to this school, but I draw the line at this . . . this *junk*."

The principal was pointing at several piles of technology: **Doc's inventions!** In between the thingamajigs and whozawhatsits, Harper and Theo spotted a pair of their old VR goggles, one of the Stonesword Library's computer monitors, *and* the server that hosted their Minecraft world. It was all there!

"That's not junk!" Theo grumbled. "That's our stuff!"

Doc Culpepper and Ms. Minerva had fought before about Doc's inventions, but Ms. Minerva had never seemed this *mad*. And Doc had never seemed this nervous before. Harper had looked up to Doc for a long time—she was Harper's favorite teacher, after all, and a brilliant scientist.

If Doc had kept that stuff, then Theo was right. **None of it was junk.** But next to all the fancy, clean computers arranged in neat rows in the Ironsword computer lab, it did *look* like junk.

"Every object here is part of various ongoing research projects and is highly important to Woodsword school business. We can't keep everything at Woodsword because my lab was

damaged." Doc tugged at the goggles on her head in a nervous way. "And my house is already so full it could burst!"

"Well, it all needs to be thrown out. This is not a *storage unit*, Dr. Culpepper. It's not a *locker* or a *very large box*. It's not *the cloud*, or a *warehouse*, or some kind of *depot*. This is a *school computer lab*."

Theo frowned. **"This guy really likes listing things."**

"We have to do something!" Harper didn't like to stand by if she could help someone with a problem. That was why she liked science: one of its core ideas was that there was always room for improvement—and *always* a way to help.

Harper had an idea. She pushed the door open and led Theo inside with a big smile on her face.

"Doc! You saved my project!" She rushed past the arguing adults to the piles of inventions and picked up the goggles, holding them above her head proudly. **"I thought it was destroyed in the storm!"**

Both Doc and the principal looked surprised to see her. Before anyone could say anything, Theo grabbed a random who-knows-what from the pile and held it up.

"And mine!" he declared. Whatever it was started glowing.

Principal Ferris was the first to speak. "Your . . . project?"

"That's right!" Harper smiled big and tried to sound as serious and scientific as she could. "We believe we've discovered a unique kind of artificial intelligence that formed by analyzing data in a piece of technological entertainment. My friends and I, under Doc's guidance, are learning all about how it works."

"And mine is blue!" Theo added.

"Which of course means . . . according to my hypothesis . . . that it is . . . a code matrix—" He paused. **"Something we are still figuring out!** Which is why it needs to stay!"

Doc Culpepper looked as if she was trying not to laugh, but she nodded and followed their lead. "Many of these items are very important to students from Woodsword. I wanted to bring them here so they could keep the ones that mattered to them."

Principal Ferris seemed unconvinced, but at least a little less angry than he had been a moment before. "I can give you one week to return things to the students. Most of these devices look water-damaged, outdated, or far too . . . *mysterious*. Like whatever that boy is holding. It doesn't look safe."

Theo waved his glowing blue object around. **A few sparks came out of one end.**

Doc winced. "Yes, Theo, you should probably set that one down."

He did.

"Whatever is still here this weekend is getting thrown out. That's my final word on the subject." Principal Ferris looked down at them. "Theo, was it? And . . . ?"

"Harper," Harper said. "Harper Houston."

The principal nodded. "I've got my eye on you two. Don't make a mess of my school."

Harper got a little chill when he said that. It felt like he meant it.

Doc Culpepper shook her head as he left. "I appreciate the help, but you really shouldn't lie to the principal, okay?"

Harper insisted, "Everything I said was true—"

Just then, Morgan, Jodi, and Po arrived, **and they were just as excited as Harper was to see the pile of so-called junk.**

"Our computers!" Morgan exclaimed.

"Our monitors!" Jodi added, hugging the slightly water-damaged screen.

"And our goggles!" Po grabbed another pair from the pile and put them over his eyes. "Hmm. The Overworld is darker than I remember."

Doc Culpepper sighed. "That's the bad news. I can't get them working. Whatever happened in there during the storm completely fried them, and

I didn't make any blueprints."

Harper was disappointed, but she understood. The big storm in the real world hit at the same time that a *data* storm hit in their Minecraft world. A major glitch they called the Fault ripped apart the version of Minecraft that had grown out of Doc's AI and Theo's tampering with the code, and only putting the Evoker King back together had stopped the Fault from erasing everything. **Now Minecraft was all the way back to normal,** but the VR goggles had been through a lot.

"So we can't play?" Morgan asked.

"That's the good news!" Doc Culpepper smiled. "The server is on, and it works with my other computers as well as the school's. I'm not sure what you kids did in there, but there's been some *very* strange activity." Doc checked her watch and walked back over to her desk. "If I didn't know better, I'd say someone is playing from the inside."

"The Evoker King!" Theo whispered. "Or . . . whoever he is now. The Evoker . . . Kid?"

Po looked confused. **"But how do we play**

without the goggles?"

That, Harper understood.

"The old-fashioned way!" she said, pulling a chair in front of the pile of junk. She connected a monitor to a

computer tower. "We can't let this stop us from seeing our friend."

Theo nodded and started helping right away. The two of them were the biggest tech whizzes on the team. Ironsword's computer lab had a supply of nice headsets: **headphones with attached microphones to keep their hands free while they typed.** Theo collected a set for each of them and plugged them in.

Jodi and Morgan pushed two large computer lab tables together to make a square, and soon they had five monitors connected to five computer towers in the center, which were each connected to the server. Each player got a different side of the table except for Morgan and Jodi, who shared a side. Harper connected the final cords, and each station hummed as it turned on.

"The Evoker Kid's been alone in there for a while." Jodi had been worried about him since their last visit. "I hope he's okay."

"I'm sure he is!" Morgan said. "And if not, we're coming to save him!"

Chapter 3

SKELETONS ARE SO HEARTLESS. AND BRAINLESS. AND LUNGLESS. BUT THEY DEFINITELY HAVE A SPINE!

Everybody put on a headset and logged in together. When the world finished loading, Morgan was surprised to find himself already inside a house! It was made of spruce and had six beds, a crafting table, a torch for light, and a chest.

He couldn't help himself. He opened the chest. Inside were five copies of every stone tool!

"Look!" Morgan called to his friends. **"THERE'S ONE HERE FOR EACH OF US."**

They crowded around the chest. "Are you sure these are ours?" Harper asked.

"Gotta be!" In the real world, Po stroked his

chin like a villain in a movie. "And if they aren't, we'll be pulling off *the crime of the century*!"

"They're only stone tools," Theo pointed out. "We can replace them if they're not meant for us."

"UH . . . I THINK YOU SHOULD ALL SEE THIS." Jodi had already opened the door. Morgan followed her outside and saw what she meant.

They were high up. *Way* up. The server was different than it had been before: their spawn point was on top of a giant spruce tree!

"Oh yeah, I remember this!" Theo said. "THE RESET GAVE US A NEW SEED."

Po shook his head. "I think a tree this big is probably a very *old* seed."

"He means the *world* seed." Harper was walking

around the house, looking out in every direction. The tall tree let her see far, even to the edge of the taiga biome. "Every time you make a new world, it creates a random string of numbers called a seed. If it's different, then everything really is reset. **NOTHING AROUND HERE IS THE WAY IT USED TO BE.**"

Morgan had something else on his mind. Someone had already built a house here. They were on top of a tree, which meant it was a *tree house.* And if he was right, a cool tree house must mean—

"ASH!" Jodi yelled, pointing down at the ground. **"SHE'S ALREADY HERE!"**

Morgan found a set of stairs built around the trunk of the tree. He rushed down, and the others followed close behind.

Ash Kapoor went to another school now, but she had been part of their Minecraft team from the beginning. She was a Wildling Scout and was almost always in her scout uniform. She had tons of merit badges to show how hard she worked at camping, hiking, swimming, building, leading . . . most importantly, though, she was a great friend.

"Hi, everyone!" Ash's Minecraft skin looked like a Wildling Scout, too. It was a surprise to hear her voice in the headset. "DOC SENT ME EVERYTHING I NEEDED TO KEEP PLAYING WITH YOU."

"I'm so glad," Morgan said. "After the Fault reset our server, and the storm reset our *school,* I don't know if I can handle any more changes."

Ash handed him a brown mushroom sympathetically. "I know what that's like. Moving would have been even harder for me if I didn't have all of you to play with."

"How did you already build all this?" Theo asked. "Aren't you in school, too?"

Ash paused. "Oh, I guess I had some extra—"

Rattle-rattle.

Uh-oh. Everybody knew that sound: a skeleton.

Thwip. Thunk.

A skeleton shooting arrows!

"Ow!" came a voice from the distance. *Thwip. Thunk.* "Ow! What an interesting experience!"

Everybody looked at each other in surprise.

Another voice?

Rattle. Thwip. Thunk. "Ow! Nice aim, buddy!"

Morgan pulled out his wooden sword and ran toward the sound and found what he was looking for—the Evoker Kid! The boy looked like a cute, short evoker, with a big nose and even bigger eyebrows.

He also had three arrows sticking out of his side.

"It is the Morgan!" a voice exclaimed in their headsets—a different voice than the Evoker King's. It sounded like a boy their age, crystal clear, like he was standing right next to them. He said every syllable slowly and perfectly, though, which was the most robot-like thing about him. "The Morgan has returned at last! Did you bring a Jodi, or perhaps a Po?"

"Yeah, they're all here." *Rattle-rattle.* "But I think you've got bigger problems!"

The skeleton was right behind the kid—wearing a complete set of golden armor!

"How did this skeleton get armor?!" Morgan asked. *Thwip*. He pushed the Evoker Kid out of the way. *Thunk*. The arrow landed in a tree behind them.

"I FOUND IT IN A BOX. Did you know you can pick things up and then drop them?"

Morgan was stunned. "You *gave armor to a skeleton?*"

"The blocks making up its body seemed incomplete without it."

"How many hearts do you have?"

The boy sounded confused. "Hearts?"

Morgan didn't have any more time to waste. He jumped forward with his sword and began swinging at the skeleton to get its attention. His sword wouldn't do much damage through that armor, but he could at least distract it from hurting the Evoker Kid any more.

Ash understood what Morgan was asking, at least. "He's asking about your health. **DO YOU SEE THE HEARTS AT THE BOTTOM OF YOUR SCREEN?"**

"My . . . screen?"

Thwip. The skeleton still wasn't paying attention to Morgan. He had to jump in front of the arrows to protect the Kid. *Thunk.* There went two hearts.

"He can't see his hearts because he's not playing the game like we are!" Harper realized. "He's *in* the game—like we used to be. He can feel it."

Thwip. Thunk.

"Then . . . how do you feel?" Po asked. "On a scale from 'so alive you could dance' to . . . 'mummy barely walking around'?"

Thwip. Thunk. "Can we figure out a plan, please?" Morgan asked, keeping the skeleton away as best as he could.

"I hadn't noticed, but now that you mention it," the boy said, "on a twenty-point scale of mummy to dancing, I would estimate I am at a one, very close to mummy."

Po gasped. **"THAT'S HALF A HEART!"**

Thwip. Thunk.

"Go hide in the tree house!" Morgan insisted. "Help me trap it!"

Jodi and Po nudged the Evoker Kid away while Theo, Harper, and Ash started placing blocks around the skeleton. Morgan held it in place by standing in the way, so it switched to hitting him directly with the bow. *Another heart gone. And another.* Now Morgan only had half a heart, too!

"Almost there!" Ash said. Just two blocks left. She placed one by its feet and went to place the last by its head—

Too late.

Thunk. Morgan flashed red. He dropped to zero hearts, and for him, the entire game froze.

"Morgan! Sorry to interrupt." Ms. Minerva was at the door of the computer lab, smiling. Morgan took off his headset so he could hear. "Could you come with me for a few minutes? **The baron and the duchess are . . . well, they're having some trouble.**"

"**Wha—?!**" Morgan barely heard Ms. Minerva at first. He couldn't remember the last time he'd died in Minecraft! Especially at the hands of a *skeleton*. He was embarrassed and wanted to jump back in right away—but then she mentioned the baron and the duchess.

Baron Sweetcheeks and **Duchess Dimples** were the hamsters that used to live at Woodsword Middle School and Stonesword Library. Morgan had had no clue that they'd been moved to Ironsword, too!

He looked back at his friends.

"Don't worry!" Harper smiled. **"WE'LL LOOK OUT FOR HIM.** The skeleton's stuck now."

As he stood up, Morgan noticed something strange. Instead of the typical *You Died!* message, the game had sent him back to the server login screen. The word **⟨ERROR⟩** flashed on the screen. *Weird,* he thought.

And he had a feeling that where the Evoker King was involved—even if he seemed to be gone now—**things would only get weirder.**

Chapter 4

IF THERE ARE TWO MUSHROOMS IN YOUR STEW, ADD SOMETHING TO FILL THE BOWL!

Theo really wanted to know what the Evoker Kid *was*. He wasn't the Evoker King, at least not exactly. He had some form of the Evoker King's data and knew the names of everything in Minecraft, but he didn't know about the outside world, or remember anything from before the server reset.

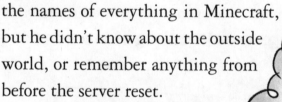

He also barely knew how to play Minecraft.

"I was out collecting red mushrooms when you all arrived," Ash said. "So we can make some stew to heal you up!" When she opened the crafting table, the Evoker Kid gasped.

"What are all those *squares*?"

"YOU CAN SEE MY CRAFTING MENU?"

"Sometimes," the Evoker Kid replied. "But only if I really focus."

"Interesting," Ash said. "The crafting menu is where you put materials if you want to craft stuff. See?" She placed a brown mushroom, a red mushroom underneath it, and a bowl underneath that. **Then she pulled mushroom stew from the table.**

"Here, eat this." Ash handed the bowl to the Evoker Kid. His blocky features suggested a pleased smile.

"Go on, eat it!" Theo said.

The Evoker Kid looked at him, confused. "How do I do that?"

This would be harder than they thought.

"If it is like how it works for us, then you just kind of . . . hold it up to your face. Like this." Theo crafted another mushroom stew and ate it in front of the Kid.

The boy lifted the stew to his face, tilted it slightly—and it disappeared. **"OH! NOW I AM FOUR-TENTHS FULL."**

Harper laughed. "That's very specific. But at least you're able to keep track of your hunger."

All this made Theo think even harder. If the Evoker Kid had health, and hunger, then he really was a player—not a mob, like skeletons or Evokers. But he wasn't a human. He didn't know how to eat, and he wasn't using a computer monitor. Yet the Evoker Kid could see other people's menus, which meant he could maybe see some other things regular players *couldn't* see. He was *inside* the server and was experiencing the world like they had with Doc's goggles.

"WHAT IS YOUR NAME?" Ash asked.

"*My* name? I've never thought about it before." The Evoker Kid frowned. "Usually when I think about something, I know what it is called. It's not like that when I think of myself."

"So the Evoker King didn't want you to be the same as he was." Po swapped skins into a big blue butterfly—a reference to the butterflies that had led them to the Evoker King's many pieces during their last adventure. **"YOU'RE SOMEBODY NEW!"** He wiggled his wings, and the Evoker Kid giggled.

Jodi tapped her chin. "Evoker Kid is kind of too long to say all the time. Maybe EK?"

"Ee-kay . . . ," Po tried.

Then, suddenly, he yelled—a high, shrill scream. **"EEEEEEEEEEEEEK!"** Everybody winced in their headphones. "That's my suggestion."

Theo stared at him. "A scream is your suggestion?!"

"Yep! Eek." Po shrugged. "I think it's cute."

"It's definitely easier to say," Jodi admitted. "When you're not screaming." She turned to the

Evoker Kid. "What do you think?"

"EEEEEEEEEEEEEEEK!" the Kid yelled, mimicking Po. Everybody was surprised except Po, who started laughing.

Theo was starting to get nervous. Human or not, Eek—as he was now named—seemed like a person. He was laughing at Po's jokes and had an opinion about his name. He trusted them, and the Evoker King had trusted them to take care of him. Even if he was just code, he was also their friend. But did that mean they were responsible for taking care of him? **What did the Evoker King expect them to do?**

Eek had never been in another world. Minecraft was all he knew. And if he only existed inside the server . . .

Theo looked over the table at Harper in the real world. She looked concerned, which meant she was thinking the same thing he was.

"WE HAVE BAD NEWS," Theo said.

"About the server," Harper said. They explained what Principal Ferris had said: At the end of the week, *all* of Doc's old experiments would be thrown out. Which meant the *server* was going to get thrown away.

"What happens to Eek if the server is *disconnected*?"

Theo didn't know. **"MAYBE HE'LL BE FINE, BUT . . ."**

"I'll be alone." Eek looked at all of them, and his face turned sad for the first time since they'd met him. "I do not want to be alone again. I want to always be with a Po, and a Jodi, and all the rest of you."

"We want that too, buddy." Ash moved over next to Eek and handed him another bowl of stew

for comfort. "No matter what, you won't end up alone. We promise."

Harper looked over at Theo again, more confident this time. Theo nodded. They would come up with a plan. **No matter what.**

Chapter 5

THE ROYAL TITLES OF HAMSTERS ARE A DELICATE AFFAIR. DON'T MESS THEM UP IF YOU WANT AN INVITATION TO THE BALL!

The Ironsword Academy's library was right next door. Ms. Minerva led Morgan there while she explained the situation.

"I've tried *everything*!" she said. "I've given them their favorite treats. They have clean wheels, new beds, and fresh water, but none of it is working. **They're not happy.**"

The hamster cages were set next to each other on a table in the back of the room, behind the encyclopedias. Morgan inspected their plastic

habitats. The duchess had buried herself in a pile of food and woodchips. The baron was lying on his back on a mound of wood shavings, staring out at Morgan with a sad look in his eyes.

"Did you try putting them in their hamster balls?" Morgan asked.

"Yes. Watch." Ms. Minerva reached in to pick up Baron Sweetcheeks and placed him in a hamster ball on the floor. He sniffed around for a second, then flopped down to take a nap without walking anywhere. "I don't know what's wrong! They were always fine with moving to different rooms before. And they love exploring!"

While Morgan was thinking, a group of students on the other side of the library all started chattering at once. "Awww, look at him! He's so cute!"

He looked toward the front of the library, by the check-out desk, and saw a crowd of Ironsword students around a *different* cage. The cage was bigger, and it was decorated with a castle-shaped hideaway. There were balls and other toys to play with as well as ample shavings and grass to eat.

"That's Prince Pellets," Ms. Minerva explained. "The Ironsword guinea pig. He's still a baby, so he's only a little bigger than the hamsters, but he'll grow to be more than twice their size one day."

Prince Pellets wiggled. The students all cheered again. The Ironsword librarian quickly shushed them, but their gleeful murmuring could still be heard across the room.

"They must really love him," Morgan said. "But nobody else is over here with the hamsters."

"Everyone's allowed to choose where they sit for reading club. They all want to be near Prince Pellets."

Morgan lifted the baron out of his ball and nuzzled his nose. He found a sunflower seed in the cage and offered it as a snack. "I like you, Baron. I'd come sit with you."

The hamster seemed to appreciate Morgan's attention and sniffed at the sunflower seed. He reached up with both paws and grabbed it.

The hamsters' mood reminded Morgan of how he'd felt when Ash joined their school. Or when Theo joined their team. Or *now,* if he was honest. Morgan knew the Evoker Kid was going to be a good friend, but the little guy—and the hamsters were—feeling the same way he used to: afraid that he'd be left behind.

"I think they miss the attention," Morgan said to Ms. Minerva. He picked up the duchess and gave her a little hug.

"Eat the grass! Eat the grass! Eat the grass!" the students chanted on the other side of the library. Prince Pellets quickly nibbled away at a small bunch of grass. The students murmured loudly again in approval.

Both hamsters turned away from the sound, then flopped onto their bellies in a huff. Morgan set them back into their cages.

Ms. Minerva sighed. "Thank you for trying, Morgan."

He didn't feel good just leaving them like this, but he needed to check on the Evoker Kid. "We'll find a way to cheer them up."

What he didn't tell Ms. Minerva was that he also needed to cheer *himself* up. What if everybody stopped caring about Morgan now that there was a new, cool AI friend to talk to?

Jodi would say he was being silly. But was he?

Chapter 6

IT'S TIME FOR SOME THEO-RISING. AND, UH, HARPER-RISING. WE'RE THINKING, OKAY?

With the skeleton contained, Theo and Harper needed to talk to Doc. Their science teacher was sorting through her experiments. The keep pile was already stacked high. The toss pile only had one thing in it: the who-knows-what that Theo had picked up before. **It was still glowing blue.**

"How's it going, Doc?" Harper asked.

"Fine." Doc set down a microwave with a big satellite dish on the top in the keep pile. "I'm thinking about what to do with these experiments. **I hate to throw anything out.**"

"Why does Principal Ferris get to decide what's

junk and what's not?" Theo grumbled.

Doc smiled. "We're guests here. **Still, I have a feeling we'll figure it out.** Was there something you wanted to talk about?"

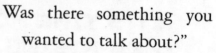

Harper nodded. "We want to ask you about the server. Is there any way to put its contents on the computers at this school?"

"One of us could take it home, but . . ." Theo frowned. "We want everybody to get to play. And there's something on this server we really don't want to lose."

Doc looked apologetic. "I've already tried. Something in the data won't let me copy or edit anything. Ash can use the internet to connect *in*, but the game won't connect *out* at all. The buttons to turn it off don't even work!"

Their Minecraft world was hosted in a large cube-shaped server with wires running to each computer they were using to play. **Doc pushed the power button a few times,** but nothing happened. "I thought that was strange. But I knew the server was important to you, so I used a portable battery to keep it running on the trip here."

"So we don't know what happens if it loses power," Harper said.

"Which means it's dangerous to move around," Theo added. All three of them were quiet for a moment as they thought about the problem.

"Why do we think the server's acting so strange?" Harper asked.

"The storm?" Doc offered as she returned to her sorting.

"Or the Fault," Theo mumbled as his own mind tracked down possibilities.

Or the Evoker King did it on purpose! Harper realized. She grabbed Theo and led him over to the other side of the computer lab.

Theo listened as Harper explained her idea. "Why would he trap Eek in there forever?"

"Maybe it isn't forever. Eek is new, right? He's

55

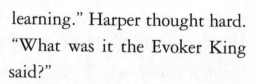

learning." Harper thought hard. "What was it the Evoker King said?"

"He said, 'I wish to experience Minecraft from a new perspective.'"

"And Eek *is* that new perspective."

"So if the Evoker King is stopping Eek from leaving the game on purpose, whatever lets him leave must be hiding in Minecraft somewhere."

Theo tried to think about the game from the Evoker King's perspective. The Evoker King was a program, which meant Theo needed to think like a programmer.

Minecraft was *huge.* There were so many things to do, and so many ways to play. You could spend years building or exploring. They only had a week.

"In video games, when you want to have something happen at a certain time, you make a trigger," Theo thought out loud. "You can start a song whenever a character says a certain line or have an achievement unlock whenever you collect one hundred items."

Po pulled one side of his headset off and called

to his friends. "Harper and Theo, you should come over here!"

Theo nodded. "One second, Po. **If the Evoker King left behind a way for Eek to leave the server, it's probably a trigger like that.**"

"And it has to be something we wouldn't do right away." Harper tried to think. Mine down to bedrock? Visit the Nether? "Something that meant we'd seen everything. Something like—"

"**The End!**" Theo exclaimed suddenly.

"There's no end in Minecraft, though." Harper shook her head. "You can do things forever!"

"No, not the end of Minecraft. The End! The dimension where you battle the Ender Dragon and see the credits. **We've never been there before, at least not as a group.**"

Harper's eyes widened. "You're right! Traveling the Overworld is easy now, and visiting the

Nether is something we all know how to do. But the Evoker King never got to experience really *playing* Minecraft, or seeing the End. Maybe he hoped Eek would one day—and he put the trigger there somewhere. **Maybe even the credits themselves."**

Theo couldn't help but smile. "It's kind of sweet. A journey with Eek all the way through the biggest challenges in the game."

"It *would* be sweet," Harper argued, "if we didn't only have a week."

"Go as fast as we can, I guess."

"Guys!" Jodi sounded panicked. "You should really come move your avatars!"

"CREEPER!" Po yelled. "And you're just standing around!"

Harper was confused. "But we logged out!"

"Your avatars are still there!"

They rushed to their computers and opened Minecraft back up. The game gradually loaded. . . .

"Hurry! Hurry! It's going to—"

Username . . . password . . .

"—explode!"

BOOM! Looking over at Po's screen, they could see the creeper explode at the base of the tree—right where they'd left their avatars. When the cloud of smoke cleared, the little Harper and Theo

avatars were gone!

Morgan walked in just in time for the stunned silence. "Hey, everyone. **How's the Kid?**"

"He's fine," Jodi said. "But Harper and Theo . . ."

⟨ERROR⟩. When Theo tried to log into the server, a big red bar appeared, blocking him out. Theo frowned. "Hmm. **That's weird.**"

"Let me try." Harper tried to log in: **⟨ERROR⟩**.

Morgan looked nervous. But when everybody stared at him, he tried logging in, too. **⟨ERROR⟩**.

"It's not working."

Everyone tried again.

"We can't enter the game."

Chapter 7

YOU KNOW WHAT THEY SAY: SIX HEADS ARE BETTER THAN THREE. (BUT WHEN YOU ONLY HAVE THREE, YOU MAKE IT WORK!)

Harper and Theo explained their theory to the team, but Morgan could barely listen. This was the worst news ever! Playing Minecraft with his friends was the one good thing left after everything else changed. Now he couldn't even do that.

"Why is this happening?" he asked. **"Why can't we get back in?"**

Theo shrugged. "It has to be another one of the Evoker King's changes. I can't see why he'd think it was a good idea, though."

Everyone was sitting at their computers, headsets on, so Ash and Eek could hear what they were talking about. Morgan sighed. "So if you two are right, our best chance at fixing this is still to get to the End. *In a week.* With only half of our team."

"We think so," Harper said. "Who has been to the End before? And fought the Ender Dragon?"

Harper, Theo, and Morgan said yes. "Not me," said Ash. Jodi and Po shook their heads.

"I USUALLY PLAY IN CREATIVE MODE," Jodi explained.

"And I'm a busy man," Po said, shrugging.

Morgan groaned. Everybody who had been to the End before was kicked out of the game!

This isn't fair, he thought. He'd beaten the Ender Dragon a dozen times. He'd made it to the credits by himself! And now because of one hostile mob, he couldn't play and he couldn't help his friends. **They needed him! Didn't they?**

Ash could tell the mood of the group was turning sour, even over headset. She tried to focus on the problem. "We've got five days, including today, to get to the End. If we don't . . . something bad might happen to Eek when the server gets taken away. That means we need a plan."

"We can make a plan!" Theo said. "But student clubs are allowed to stay until five o'clock, so we have over an hour left."

Harper nodded. "Morgan, can you answer questions and keep an eye on everybody while we figure it out?"

He didn't want to. He thought about defeating the Ender Dragon again. He wanted to *play*. But if Harper and Theo didn't want his help, then babysitting was the best he could do. "Sure. Whatever."

Everybody could tell he was upset. And nobody knew what to say. After a quiet moment, Eek finally spoke.

"I AM NOT SURE WHAT IS GOING ON," he said. "You do not need to go to all this trouble for me."

"Yes, we do," Jodi replied. "You're part of our team. We're not leaving you behind."

Yeah, just me, Morgan thought.

"But I am the cause of your problems. If it was not for me, you would be enjoying your game like normal."

"IT'S NOT SO SIMPLE," Jodi said. "We all make mistakes, and we all end up in bad situations. When you're part of a team, it's everybody's job to help."

"All this makes my head hurt!" Po said.

"Me too," Ash admitted. "Jodi's right, Eek. Let us help you. We want to."

Eek considered this for a moment. "Thank you, friends. **I WAS TRYING TO BE BRAVE, BUT I DO NOT WANT TO BE LEFT ALONE."**

Me neither, Morgan thought. But he already felt like he would be. Harper and Theo would make their plan together, Jodi and Po would take care of Eek, and Ash would be the *real* leader. Maybe all he was good for was getting hit with arrows.

"SO WHAT'S OUR FIRST GOAL?" Ash asked. "What do we need to get to the End?"

Harper didn't even pause. "Same as usual. Which means—"

"Obsidian," Morgan grumbled.

Chapter 8

IF YOU CAN'T BEAT THEM . . . BUILD THEM A PLACE TO LIVE AND MAKE SURE THEY'RE COMFORTABLE.

"These are the basic tools." Po placed one of each tool on the ground: a pickaxe, an axe, a sword, a shovel, and a hoe. "The sword is actually a weapon, but it's just as important."

Eek took the pickaxe and held it in his hand. **"HOW INTERESTING!"** he said. He dropped it back down on the ground.

"No, keep it! I'm going to show you how to use it."

"Very well." Eek picked it back up. "I do not know what I would need to use it for. I already know how to pick things up and put them back down. See?"

Po laughed. "You can do way more than that!" Po took out his own pickaxe and walked over to a nearby hill of exposed stone. He gave it a few good *thwack*s with the pickaxe, and a block popped out of the hill and floated into the air. Eek gasped.

"Now you can pick *that* up and put it down."

"Why?"

"TO MAKE THINGS YOU WANT TO MAKE."

"Like what?"

"Like Ash's tree house. Anything."

"Hmm . . ." Eek looked unconvinced as he picked up the block of stone.

"NOW PUT IT BACK DOWN SOMEWHERE YOU WANT IT TO GO."

Eek placed it back into the hill.

"Somewhere else, I mean!"

"I LIKE IT BEST RIGHT THERE."

Po shrugged. "If you say so. How about you try now?"

"Try what?"

"Breaking a stone block."

"Why would I do that?"

"To put it somewhere else."

"I LIKE WHERE IT IS!"

Po had never needed to explain something so basic before—but Ash and Jodi had put him in charge of teaching Eek while they mined for iron, so he had to try. "Sometimes you need to build something to keep yourself safe, or to keep animals from wandering away, or to trap a mob. Remember when we covered the skeleton up with stones?"

"THE SKELETON!" Eek gasped again, suddenly remembering. He ran away immediately! Po chased him to where random blocks were still placed in an uneven cocoon jutting out of the ground. He could still hear the *rattle-rattle* from behind the rock.

"Once we have better weapons, we can destroy it and get your armor back."

"NO!" Eek sounded horrified. **"PLEASE DO NOT! IT IS MY FRIEND!"**

"It was trying to kill you with its bow, Eek!"

The boy shook his head. "I understand. But when I was by myself, the skeleton followed me. We were exploring together." He looked at the pile of stone. *Rattle-rattle.* "It must feel very alone inside there."

Po didn't know what to say to that. The skeleton was a hostile mob, and that meant it was bad news. But if Eek wanted to keep it . . . **That gave him an idea.** "I think we could build a place to keep your skeleton safe but not so alone, if you want."

With a quick spin of his mouse wheel in the real world, Po was now holding an axe. "We'll need wood. **GRAB YOUR AXE AND MEET ME OVER BY THOSE TREES."** Spruce blocks popped out with just a few hits. "We'll need a bunch, so you work on chopping blocks from the other one."

"No, thank you." Eek shook his head.

Po sighed. "What is it this time?"

"I like the tree. **I DO NOT WANT TO DESTROY IT."**

"We have to! We need wood to build a fence."

"Then I do not want to build a fence."

"If we don't build a fence," Po explained patiently, "we have to leave your skeleton inside the stones."

"But we cannot leave the skeleton in the stones."

"You know, when I play Minecraft by myself, my favorite part is exploring. I like meeting animals and bringing them along with me as I explore. I like building tiny bases all over the place, not really making giant builds or trying to get to the End. **I THINK MINECRAFT IS BEAUTIFUL AS**

Eek nodded. "There is so much to explore. So much that is already beautiful. Why would I want to destroy it?"

Po looked up at the giant spruce. Eek was right. The sun was just starting to set, and the colors of the sky met the leaves of the tree to create a very beautiful picture on his monitor. He took a screenshot so he wouldn't forget.

"THE IMPORTANT THING, IN ANY WORLD, IS TO GIVE BACK SOMETHING FOR EVERYTHING YOU TAKE." Po gestured to the blocks he'd already taken from the spruce. "We *will* have to chop down some trees, but we can make something beautiful in exchange. And as for the tree . . ." Po remembered a detail he'd almost forgotten about Minecraft trees. "You don't have to chop this one down—**I'LL DO IT.** But you have to trust me that it'll be okay."

Eek considered. After a moment, he nodded. Po grinned and then, in a flash, chopped down one of the spruce trees—all of it. Logs, leaves, everything. At the end, he checked his inventory: four saplings had dropped from the leaves. *Perfect.*

"THE TREE IS GONE, but we can make another one. Here, take these." He handed all four saplings to Eek. "Put them down next to each other, where the tree was before."

Eek, already an expert in putting things down, placed the four saplings in a square. He gasped. **"LITTLE TREES!"**

"Yes! Little trees! And they'll grow into big

ones eventually." Po swapped over to the hoe tool. "*This* tool is also for growing. You can plant seeds to grow crops for food, and for other stuff."

"I see!" **Eek held up his stone hoe.** "Then this is the only tool I will need."

"That wasn't—" Po shook his head and laughed. "Okay, sure. If you say so."

Po crafted a bunch of fences, then surrounded the skeleton's stone cage with a fence three blocks high and a gate. "I'm going to let it out with the pickaxe," Po warned. **"YOU DON'T WANT YOUR SWORD, RIGHT?"**

Eek nodded.

"Then when I let the skeleton out, give it your sword like you did with the armor. If we're lucky, it'll drop the bow and I can get the bow out of there."

Po was nervous, but **he wanted Eek to be happy.** He was also excited. This was kind of risky!

When Po was confident Eek understood, he opened the gate. A few swings of his pickaxe revealed the skeleton, still standing there with bright golden armor. *Rattle-rattle.*

"Here you go!" Eek yelled. He threw his sword at the skeleton's feet. Po hid on the other side of the stones.

The skeleton immediately swapped its bow for

the stronger sword. Po dashed out and picked up the bow. **Sprinting, Po ran out of the gate with Eek and closed it,** leaving the armored skeleton to walk around inside its new pen.

"Now that it doesn't have a bow . . ." Po's heart was racing. Knowing that death was permanent on this server made hostile mobs extra scary. "It can't fire arrows at us. But it *can* watch us build, and you can keep an eye on it."

Eek looked at the skeleton through the fence posts. The skeleton stared back. *Rattle-rattle.* Po wondered if Eek felt like he and the skeleton were the same. They were both programs, after all. And so were the trees. If Eek was real—and Po believed he was—then all of it was real, sort of.

Real enough for Po, at least.

"We're back!" Ash called. She and Jodi ran up to see their new fence. The skeleton rattled hello.

"With all the iron we could ever need!" Jodi grinned. "Time to get crafting!"

"Just a hoe for me, please," Eek said. Ash and Jodi looked confused, but Po gave them a look that said *just go with it.*

"Let us know if you need help. But until then"—Po grinned—**"WE AND OUR SKELETON FRIEND HAVE SOME FARMING TO DO."**

Chapter 9

THEY SAY DIAMONDS ARE FOREVER BECAUSE IT TAKES FOREVER TO MINE THEM!

The first part of Harper and Theo's plan was clear: they needed obsidian *today*, before everybody left. Ironsword sent all student groups home at five . . . and the clock was ticking!

Theo and Harper kept an eye on all the equipment and started writing down a plan for the whole week. Morgan sat next to Jodi and watched, trying to give advice. **It felt strange to be split up after so many adventures together inside the game,** but at least they could all still talk to each other when their headsets were on.

"So we . . . start digging and hope we find

diamonds?" Jodi asked.

"No, they mostly appear down deep, near bedrock. You'll need to dig for a while before you start looking," Morgan said, watching Jodi's screen. "Everybody should spread out and start digging in separate places. *Not* straight down. **Make a staircase.**"

"You got it, boss." Po did a little fake salute over the table, which made Jodi laugh. Morgan didn't think it was that funny. He didn't *want* to be giving orders. He wanted to be playing! But now giving advice was all he could do, and all the advice felt basic.

Eek didn't want to smash blocks, so he was on torch duty. While Jodi dug her staircase, Eek carefully placed another light whenever they couldn't see. "I like torches," Eek said after a while. **"THEY FEEL WARM AND SAFE."**

"Mining is scary sometimes," Jodi agreed. "But the light keeps mobs away and protects us from getting lost. They feel safe to me, too."

She paused. Eek's light had revealed some iron along the wall. She mined it—but when the iron dropped, she couldn't pick it up. "Oh, my inventory's full. I'll head back to the base."

"But we—" Ash began. Jodi was already on the move. In the tree house, **she unloaded her inventory into a chest,** then rushed out again.

Jodi walked all the way back down the staircase, picked up the iron, then started digging again. Through all this, **Eek happily trotted along behind her, placing torches.**

A few layers deeper, Jodi's iron pickaxe finally broke. She checked her inventory—no pickaxes available.

"You put them back in the chest at base with your other stuff," Morgan explained.

Jodi look at him in the real world, frustrated. "If you saw that, why didn't you say anything?"

"I didn't want to be bossy."

"Is *bossy* a kind of mob?" Eek asked cheerfully.

"I DON'T THINK NOW IS A GOOD TIME,"

Po whispered to him.

"That was the whole point, right?" Jodi asked Morgan. "Harper and Theo make the plan, and you help us figure out how to *do* the plan."

"But I shouldn't have to!" Morgan complained. "Everyone knows how to mine! Or everyone *should,* at least. **You should know to bring extra tools and chests to hold materials, and to look for caves.** You should know where diamonds are! This is all basic stuff!"

Jodi frowned. Her feelings were hurt. "Maybe to *you* it is," she said. "But we don't all play Minecraft the same way. We're having to learn, just like you did."

"There's no time to learn!" Morgan yelled, not meaning to raise his voice, but he was upset, too. Upset at being kicked out of the game, at feeling useless, at feeling like he couldn't say anything right. "*I* should be doing this. I've done it a million times! **I know how to mine, I know how to find diamonds,** and I know how to beat the game. If you guys don't, then you should just let me use your character. Waiting for you is a waste of time."

Po winced. "Ouch."

"IT WASN'T OUR FAULT YOU DIED, MORGAN."

"I know, but somebody had to do *something*. It's not like Eek was going to save himself!"

"Oh, are you talking about me?" Eek said. He hadn't been listening. He'd been adding torches to every single open block around them. They were completely surrounded by light. "I am out of torches!"

"It's not Eek's fault, either! How were any of us supposed to understand what was going on? The rules are all mixed up."

"I AM A PERSON? THAT IS MOST EXCELLENT NEWS!" Eek interjected.

"This whole problem was an *accident*. We don't

know what the Evoker King was thinking, and *he* didn't know we'd have a time limit. We're all doing our best!"

Morgan crossed his arms. **"If you really want to save him, get off the computer and let me take over."**

"No," Jodi said stubornly. "I'm going to do my job, help him, and be part of a team, like I thought *we* were! If you don't want to help, then—"

"Doctor Culpepper? Are you in here?" someone interrupted, pushing the computer lab's door open. Morgan knew exactly who it was. **Sharp hair, sharp tie, sharp tilt to his eyebrows:** Principal Ferris.

The principal had given them one week because they'd agreed to take Doc's experiments home, not rearrange the whole computer lab to play Minecraft! Eek's situation was far too complicated—and unbelievable—to explain. Someone needed to make sure he didn't see what they were doing.

Morgan didn't hesitate.

"Principal Ferris!" He threw off his headset and moved to the door as fast as he could. "Doc left

for a minute, but I had something I *really* wanted to ask you about. It's in the library, if you don't mind."

"I'm a very busy man," Principal Ferris warned. "I don't have time for frivolous concerns."

"Oh, it's not frivolous at all!" Morgan squeezed between Principal Ferris and the door, shutting it behind him. **"It concerns the health and well-being of our school pets."**

"Very well," Principal Ferris said, "let's hear it."

Morgan let out a sigh of relief. He couldn't look back at his friends, and he knew he would have to finish talking to Jodi at some point . . . **but protecting Eek was more important** than arguing about *who* would protect him.

Chapter 10

IT'S CALLED BEDROCK BECAUSE WHEN YOU GET THERE, YOU'LL NEED SOME REST FROM ALL THE DIGGING!

Jodi swung her pickaxe so wildly that Eek stood a few blocks away just in case. "Where . . . *are they?*" she yelled, clicking and swinging and clicking and swinging.

She, Ash, and Po had all made it to the best depth for diamonds, and now they had to dig tunnels in all directions, searching for deposits. Jodi was determined to get obsidian before Morgan came back, to prove she could handle the job as well as he could.

Jodi said in her best leader voice, **"WE'LL FIND DIAMONDS SOON."**

Eek spoke up. **"JODI, I BELIEVE THIS IS**

ALL MY FAULT AGAIN."

"Huh? No. It's not your fault." She paused for a moment to break a block of iron, then kept moving. "Morgan's just in a bad mood."

Eek dodged the swinging pickaxe but stayed close enough to talk to her. "You do not seem to be in a good mood, either."

Jodi didn't want to keep talking about it, but because he was in Minecraft, Eek couldn't see her I-don't-want-to-keep-talking-about-it face in the real world. "Po said Morgan is your brother. What is this?"

"It means we have the same parents. We live in the same house."

"SO YOU ARE NEVER ALONE."

Jodi hadn't thought about it that way before. "No, I guess not. He's older than me, so we weren't always like this. I skipped a grade. So now we live in the same house, go to the same classes, **AND PLAY MINECRAFT TOGETHER. . . ."** She shrugged. "But we're still different people."

"And because you are different, and you are never alone, you disagree."

Jodi nodded. "I guess so."

Eek thought about this and said, "I suppose the skeleton is my brother."

"What?!"

"We were both created in Minecraft. We live in the same base. We do not agree on whether arrows should be fired at friends."

"EEK, I KNOW YOU LIKE THE SKELETON, but the skeleton wants to hurt you because it's programmed that way. Even when we fight, Morgan and I don't want to *hurt* each other. Arrows are different from disagreements."

He looked genuinely confused. "IF YOU DO NOT WANT TO HURT EACH OTHER, WHY DO YOU FIGHT?"

Jodi looked across the table at Po for help. He pretended he didn't see—and Ash wasn't talking, either. Nobody wanted to help her explain this to Eek. **Or maybe they knew it would be good for her to work through it.**

"Morgan is always like this. He's good at a lot of things, but not very good at sharing—especially what he is thinking. When we fight, it's usually because he's gotten upset about something he hasn't even explained. And today . . . if I'm not the *best* at something, I still want to *try*. HE ALWAYS WANTS TO BE THE BEST. Even if it means getting mad at himself or his teammates."

She sighed and added, "And he can just be so *rude* about it!"

Ash laughed. "Do you remember when I first moved here? He was rude to me, too. But he apologized later."

Jodi kept swinging at the wall. "I guess."

"AND WHEN WE NEEDED HELP TO SAVE THE EVOKER KING! He agreed to let all your classmates help us, even if it meant he might be less important."

Jodi paused, listening. "Yeah, okay."

"HE JUMPED IN TO SAVE EEK, a new member of our team, right away. And when Principal Ferris came in just now, he put everything aside to protect us."

"Okay! I get it!" Jodi huffed.

Ash laughed again—but not a mean laugh. "You two really are alike. But I think Morgan is scared more than he is mad."

"HE DOES NOT WANT TO BE ALONE," Eek said. "And because he saved me, he is."

Jodi had stopped mining completely to talk. "No, he's not! We are all right here! I'm *glad* he saved you, Eek! I *do* feel bad about it! But . . ."

Ash finished the sentence for her. "But you

want a chance to be important, too."

Jodi's voice was quiet. "Yeah. I do. Thank you, Ash."

"No problem! **THIS IS HOW I GOT MY PEER MEDIATION BADGE.**"

Jodi picked up her pickaxe again. She hit the blocks in front of her—

Eek honked in surprise. A soft red glow filled the space in front of them—a pool of lava! They stepped through the crack.

It was the biggest cave Jodi had ever seen. And it was just a few levels above bedrock, which meant there were probably a *ton*

of diamonds lurking around the cave's curves and corners.

But first, there was something she needed to do. "We found a cave!"

"Finally!" Po groaned.

"I'm building a place for Eek and me to hide," Jodi said. "Can you all protect him while I go do something?"

"Of course!" Ash said. "We'll be right there."

Chapter 11

THERE'S HONOR IN BECOMING A GUINEA PIG'S KNIGHT. AND EVEN MORE HONOR IN APOLOGIZING!

"As you can see," Morgan explained, "the hamsters seem a little lonely. I was wondering if you had any advice for—"

"The solution is simple." Principal Ferris peered at the duchess. **"They should be sent somewhere else."**

Morgan froze in surprise. **"They ... what?"**

"The purpose of a school pet is to provide joy to the students. And *comfort,* and *entertainment,* and a *sense of responsibility.* If the guinea pig is doing that better, then Prince Pellets is all we need."

This was not going how Morgan thought it would. They stood together for a

moment while Ms. Minerva's reading club turned pages on the other side of the room.

Principal Ferris demanded, "What is your name?"

"Morgan. **Morgan Mercado.**"

"I know you are new here, Morgan, but at Ironsword Academy we want only the *brightest, best,* and *most perfect* education for our students. **You and your friends will have to learn this if you want to fit in.**"

"But the baron isn't *worse* than Prince Pellets!" Morgan argued. "Prince Pellets was just here first. The students have had more time to get to know him. We should—"

"*Ahem,*" Principal Ferris interrupted Morgan, looking him directly in the eyes. "I have a question for you, Mr. Mercado. As I have just told you, we do things the *best* way here at Ironsword. Do you understand that?"

Morgan knew what the principal wanted to hear, so he said, "Yes."

"I'm so glad you said that. I'll recommend to Ms. Minerva that the hamsters be moved if they continue to be *redundant, superfluous,* and simply *extra.* They can go with all that junk in the lab." Principal Ferris turned and walked away. "First Harper, then Theo, and now you. I recommend you learn our school's rules before I have to learn any more of your names." He didn't say *or else,* but Morgan heard it loud and clear.

The principal opened the door to leave. To his surprise, he found Jodi standing on the other side, just about to walk in.

"Principal Ferris! Excuse me, I was just looking for—"

Morgan put a finger to his lips to tell her to stay quiet as the principal left the room.

Ms. Minerva's reading club was finishing the day's chapters. The students were starting to gather around Prince Pellets.

"Who's that?" Jodi asked. "He's super cute."

"*Shhh!*" Morgan shook his head. "You'll upset them." He pointed at the hamsters.

"Sorry." Jodi put on a big frown and said sarcastically. **"Who cares if he's so cute?** And has an adorable and silly crown? Who does that guinea pig think he is?"

Morgan let Baron Sweetcheeks sit on the top of his head. The baron snuggled into his hair. "I think they miss Woodsword students. Everybody *here* likes Prince Pellets."

"Then I'm upset, too."

Morgan continued. "And Principal Ferris was *no* help. He thinks they shouldn't be here at all."

He was still feeling bad about his argument with Jodi. He realized that the way he'd talked

to Jodi was a lot like the way Principal Ferris had
talked about the hamsters.

They sat in silence for a moment. Then,
suddenly, they talked at the same time:

"I'm sorry I was **so impatient.**"

"*No.* I'm sorry I was **so stubborn.**"

And then they started laughing.

"I shouldn't have gotten mad at you so fast.
You were right. It *does* make sense for you to play

my character if it'll save Eek," said Jodi.

"And I shouldn't have been so upset in the first place. It was *my* choice to jump in front of those arrows, **and it was because I wanted to be a hero.** Getting mad at you for the consequences isn't fair."

"You *are* a hero, and I think this *all* isn't fair." Jodi looked at him. "And we need you." Morgan could tell his sister was serious. "You should play my character. Eek would be better off with you as a protector."

Morgan almost agreed, but he paused. Jodi might be his little sister, but they'd been playing Minecraft together from the beginning. Just because she approached it differently didn't mean she was any *worse* at the game. **There were so many things Eek could learn from her that he wouldn't learn from Morgan.**

"No." Morgan shook his head. "I'll come back and help. But *you* should be the one to play."

"If you're sure." Jodi *did* want to play. Morgan could tell. It would be selfish to take that away from her.

"I'm sure. **We should all do what we're best at.** If I really know the most about getting to the End, it's better if I focus on guiding everybody else." He smiled. **"And someone will have to protect you all while you're playing. It's really the most important position to be in, if you think about it."**

Jodi laughed and pulled Morgan into a big hug, knowing they had both made the right decision.

On the other side of the library, the students cheered again. Morgan raised an eyebrow. One of the students was feeding fresh grass one blade at a time to Prince Pellets. The students cheered like it was the most amazing thing ever.

The duchess yawned in Jodi's hands. "We really need to do something to help the hamsters' mood," she said.

Morgan had an idea. "The hamsters want to feel special, just like we do. But no one else knows how special they are yet. They haven't had a chance to be in the spotlight."

"So we need to show them!" Jodi gasped. **"A hamster pageant!"**

Morgan grinned. "That's a great idea! Before everyone goes home—"

"We can show the reading club why we love the baron and the duchess so much!"

They put the hamsters in the baron's cage. **"We'll be right back!"**

Jodi looked at the baron very seriously. "Practice your runway walk, okay?"

He squeaked. The duchess was already trotting on the wheel—she didn't need any practice.

Morgan and Jodi then ran to the computer lab.

Chapter 12

MOSS: ONE OF THE MOST POWERFUL FORMS OF LIFE. IT CAN COMPLETELY REPLACE ROCKS IN SECONDS . . . IN MINECRAFT, AT LEAST.

A big, dark cave in Minecraft means mobs. Lots of mobs. Po and Ash had their hands full fighting creepers, skeletons, and zombies while Eek hid in the tiny hut Jodi had built for him.

They were lucky: **Jodi's long tunnel had grown a lush cave full of glow berries,** their orange light making it easier to see. Mobs hate light and stop appearing in well-lit places. But the cave was *enormous,* and a lot of it was still dark.

Ash and Po were trying to fill the darkness with torches, but every time they beat one kind of mob, another appeared. **Now it was spiders.** In real

life, Ash loved spiders. In Minecraft, she wished they would jump into lava on their own.

"What is that?" a voice behind her asked. She was surprised to see Eek standing there, and she barely jumped out of the way of the spider attack. He was pointing at a green block on the ground.

Keeuchh! The spider hissed as it leapt toward Ash. **She swung her sword down, defeating it with a final strike.**

"That's moss," Ash said. "You should really go back to the house."

"Mm," Eek said, poking the moss before wandering away. "Okay!"

Rattle-rattle. **Another skeleton!**

Po jumped in to slash first, and Ash joined a second time. Po checked over Ash's shoulder to make sure Eek wasn't watching when he defeated it, but the AI didn't seem to mind that they were fighting mobs in here.

A moment after they defeated the skeleton and placed some torches down, Eek appeared next to them again.

"DO YOU HAVE ANY MORE OF THIS THING CALLED BONE MEAL?" Eek asked.

Ash and Po looked at each other's avatars. Ash said, "Yes, we do."

"Where does it come from?"

Po shook his head vigorously behind Eek's back to signal that Ash shouldn't tell him.

Ash didn't want to make her friend sad, but she also didn't like lying. **"IT COMES FROM SKELETONS.** They drop bones when they're defeated. And we can turn it into this—bone meal."

She couldn't see Po's face in the real world, but she could hear him smack his forehead with his hand. Eek looked thoughtful.

"DEFEATED SKELETONS?"

Ash nodded. "We have to, to keep everybody safe."

Eek asked, "May I have the rest of the bone meal?"

Po gave what was in his inventory to Eek. Ash did the same. "Sure."

"Thank you," Eek said, and headed back toward the entrance again.

Ash was tired. **They'd been fighting mobs for ages in this huge place,** and each of them had only found one diamond block. She'd thought for *sure* there'd be more around here.

"I think we've got everything lit up, at least!" Po said. "Maybe Jodi will see something we missed."

Right on cue, Ash heard the jostling of headsets and two new voices in their chat.

"We're back!" Morgan said. Ash was glad to hear his voice. He sounded cheerful, too. **"Whoa . . . Eek, what did you do?!"**

Po and Ash made their way back to the first room of the lush cave. They were stunned—since they'd left, every inch of stone in the floor had been replaced with beautiful green moss blocks. Grass grew over all of it, and pink azalea bushes poked out of the ground here and there. Eek was smiling and looking proud of himself.

"I FOUND MOSS!" he said. "And I discovered a very interesting property of bone meal: when it is planted in moss, the stone blocks around it turn into *more* moss, and grass, and even little trees!"

Eek paused for a moment, gathering his thoughts. At first, Ash thought she had made a mistake. He must be *so* sad, after learning about the skeletons. "Eek, I'm sorry, I—"

"I thought maybe I should not use it. **BUT PO TOLD ME THAT WHATEVER WE TAKE WE MUST GIVE BACK.**" Eek smiled then. "I wanted to place the skeletons' seeds back in the ground, too. And look at what they have done!"

Eek didn't sound sad at all. He sounded proud. **"IT SEEMS TO ME THAT, IN MINECRAFT, SKELETONS ARE MUCH LIKE TREES.** We may have to take things from them, but we can give something back. We can make something beautiful in exchange."

"That's sweet, Eek." Ash brought her avatar over to nudge him supportively. "And exactly right."

"And GENIUS!" Morgan yelled. It was so loud everybody winced in their headsets. **"Eek, this is exactly what we needed!"**

Ash looked over at Jodi, confused.

"I dunno what he's talking about," Jodi whispered. **(Not that a whisper did much when they were all in the same voice chat.)**

"Eek, you've got your hoe, right?"

Eek held up his only tool—an iron hoe—and nodded.

Morgan had such a big smile in his voice that Ash couldn't help but smile, too.

"Then it's time to get to work. Collect that moss!"

While the others looked on expectantly, Eek seemed nervous. He wasn't sure he wanted to break the moss blocks already. He'd just put them there!

Ash nudged him forward. "You can trust Morgan," she said. "And you won't lose anything. If you have even one moss block, we can make more anywhere. EVERY BLOCK YOU BREAK RIGHT NOW IS ITS OWN FUTURE GARDEN."

When she said that, Eek's face lit up with excitement. *I'm really earning my Peer Mediation badge again today,* Ash thought.

Eek lifted his hoe—and brought it down on a moss block. The moss disappeared instantly. When he realized how fast moss blocks broke, and how quickly they entered his inventory, Eek rushed forward in perfect lines, clearing out the moss faster than any of them would have with a mouse and keyboard. **It was amazing!**

"He really is a program," Harper said. She and Theo had put headsets on, too.

"I wonder what *else* he can do," Theo said.

Just a few moments—and a couple hundred blocks of moss—later, everyone saw exactly what Morgan was talking about. With the stone out of the way, the blocks hiding underneath were all revealed.

"Diamond doesn't usually spawn in open air," Morgan explained. "It would take *forever* to break all the stone, but Eek gave us a shortcut." Now there were dozens of diamond blocks, scattered across the whole cave, glittering up at them. Enough for all their tools and then some. **"And all we needed was a hoe."**

No pickaxes broken. No blocks

wasted. And *way* faster.

"I did something good?" Eek asked.

"Very good, Eek." Ash started to believe, really believe, that they could do this. **They could reach the End in a week.**

Chapter 13

I LAVA WHEN EVERYTHING WORKS OUT. WATER YOU MEAN THAT'S HOW YOU GET OBSIDIAN?!

Someone knocked and entered the computer lab. It was a short boy in wide, round glasses and an Ironsword student council sash. **Morgan recognized him,** but he wasn't sure where they'd met before.

"Principal Ferris has asked me to remind visiting Woodsword students that all school clubs end at five o'clock *sharp*!" He blinked a few times. "Oh, hey, Po."

"Will!" Po grinned and waved to him. **"Thanks for your help today."**

"No problem." He noticed Morgan, and his smile got even bigger. "And, uh, sorry."

That's where Morgan recognized him from. He was the one who had given them the convoluted directions through Ironsword.

"**I'm Will Knight!** President of the Ironsword student council."

JODI RAISED HER EYEBROWS. "Since when does a president play pranks on the new kids?"

Will shrugged. "I was doing you a favor, really. Setting up a good surprise."

On their headsets, Eek asked, "Who are you talking to?"

"Anyway," Will continued, **"you've got a few minutes left before Principal Ferris starts shutting all the after-school activities down."**

There was no time to waste. They returned their focus to Minecraft. "The last thing we need to do is poor water on lava. Did anybody craft a bucket?"

"I did." Po held up a bucket full of water. "Morgan reminded me."

"Perfect!" Harper pointed at Po's screen so he could walk over to where he needed to pour. "Luckily, there's lava right here in this cave."

Po poured his water on the block next to the lava first—it flowed over the edge. **WHERE IT MET THE LAVA, THE TWO COMBINED AND COOLED INTO CHUNKS OF TOUGH OBSIDIAN.**

"Wow!" Eek said, reaching down to touch the new block. **"TWO THINGS COMBINING INTO SOMETHING COMPLETELY DIFFERENT."**

"If you like *that*," Po said, grinning, "you're going to love when you try cooking."

"The lava is stew?" Eek asked, taking out his bowl.

"NO!" everyone yelled.

Eek put his bowl away.

"Now use the diamond pickaxes Ash made!" Morgan ordered.

Jodi and Ash hit the obsidian blocks one by one. Po poured more water, and they harvested more obsidian. Soon they had enough for a portal.

"Now make a rectangle with them, like a doorway. You all know what a Nether portal looks like." They built it quickly: **four blocks across, five blocks high.** But Morgan stopped Jodi before she placed the final block in the top.

"We can finish it tomorrow. Eek, are you listening?"

"No." Eek was collecting lava in a bucket.

"We have to leave for today. Stay in this cave and *be careful*. Don't go through the Nether portal. It's very dangerous." Morgan paused. "Wait, did you say *no*?"

"I did." Eek filled another bucket with lava. "Should I be listening now?"

Jodi's avatar walked over to Eek and nudged him to get his attention. **"DON'T GO THROUGH THE PORTAL, OKAY?"**

Eek nodded seriously. "I understand. I will not go alone."

"Good. We'll see you soon."

Everyone said goodbye to Eek and Ash and logged out of the game.

"Since we still have a few minutes . . . ," Morgan said to Harper, Theo, and Po, **"Some of our other friends need help."**

Click! Click! Cameras snapped photos as music blasted in the library.

"Good *evening,* Ironsword reading club!" Po, holding a dry-erase marker as a microphone, raised his voice to grab the attention of all the students in the library. "It is time for the *first-ever* Sunflower Seed Ball! **The category is Fashion Ball!**"

Ms. Minerva hit the lights. Soon only one table was lit from above—Jodi was just taping down the last piece of the red construction paper runway.

Morgan placed their first star on the table: Baron Sweetcheeks. He looked a little nervous.

"Baron Sweetcheeks, a fan favorite from Woodsword Middle School, takes the red carpet in a *classic* blue hamster ball!" Po said.

Baron Sweetcheeks rolled forward a few inches in his ball. Then he rolled back a few inches. Jodi held up her phone to make a video. The baron took a moment, then proudly pushed his ball down the runway toward her. The Woodsword students cheered for him, and the

Ironsword students—who had been standing over by Prince Pellets—started walking over.

Duchess Dimples didn't wait for the baron to finish before her ball started rolling down the table. Harper and Theo held up phones and took pictures—with the flash off so they didn't scare the hamsters.

"And Duchess Dimples, sure to win Best Dressed, in her signature pink ball. A matching bow? Duchess Dimples, you have outdone yourself once *again*!"

Some of the Ironsword students cheered. At the edge of the runway,

Jodi picked up both hamster balls and brought them over to their new fans.

"Po! *Psst!*"

It was Will, the student council president. He was pointing at Prince Pellets, who was looking curiously toward the noise. "Can Prince Pellets go, too?"

Po looked at Morgan.

"Of course!" Morgan said.

Will placed Prince Pellets on the runway.

"A golden crown and a golden *treat ball*! Look at that! **The newcomer from Ironsword Academy is rolling his ball down the runway,** dispensing delicious snacks as he goes!"

Everyone cheered–Woodsword and Ironsword students alike!

Morgan felt happier than he'd felt in days.

Even with all the changes—**new school, new computer lab, new Minecraft challenges**—his friends were still his friends.

"Uh, hey." Will came over to Morgan and asked, **"Was that Minecraft you were playing?"**

"It was!" Morgan nodded. "We play whenever we can."

Will's eyes lit up. "Can I join you? Student council stuff keeps me pretty busy, but I get some days off."

Morgan froze. A new team member? Again? But this was an *Ironsword* kid, and they already had a full team, and Eek had just joined, and—

Jodi appeared behind him and nudged his shoulder. "Why not?"

Morgan couldn't help smiling. She was right. **"Honestly, we could use the help,"** Morgan said. "I hope you're ready for a *long* story."

Epilogue

THIS ONE WON'T END WITH A CLIFFHANGER. PROBABLY. IF EEK LISTENS. SURELY HE'LL LISTEN. RIGHT?

Alone again, Eek wandered. Days passed in Minecraft—sunup to sundown—and he looked for ways to pass the time. First he did what he was told: he waited in the cave.

But that quickly got boring, **so he grew more moss.**

Then *that* got boring, so he built some statues to look like his friends.

And then *that* got boring.

He went back to his friend. It only took a few hits to break a hole in the fence, but it took longer to get the skeleton to notice him. Once it did, Eek was careful to stay out of sword range as he led it away.

A few steps at a time, Eek and the skeleton went down the staircase to the portal.

He slipped the last obsidian block into place. Ash had left flint and steel in one of the chests, and Eek *had* been listening when she explained that. He carried it over to the portal.

Click. Purple ripples appeared in between the blocks. Eek stared in wonder at the light.

Rattle-rattle. "Yes, we're going." Eek smiled at his friend and casually sidestepped another sword swipe as if it were part of the conversation. "They said it was dangerous to go *alone,* so you're coming with me."

Rattle-rattle. **Eek dodged another sword swipe and chuckled at the thought of the fun they were going to have together.**

It would only be for a moment.

Eek checked his inventory: two buckets of lava, three bowls of mushroom stew, and a diamond hoe. **Everything he needed!**

Eek stepped into the portal with the skeleton following him.

And with a *whoosh* . . . Eek and his friend were gone.

INTO THE GAME!

Five young Minecraft players in the real world find themselves transported inside the game they love. But now it's not a game—and they will have to use everything they know to explore, build, and survive!

978-1-9848-5045-4 (trade) — 978-1-9848-5047-8 (ebook) — 978-0-593-40120-0 (digital audio)

NIGHT OF THE BATS!

When zombie hordes attack them in the game and bats invade their school in the real world, Ash, Morgan, and their friends realize that it's going to take all their talents to get to the bottom of these monstrous migrations.

978-1-9848-5048-5 (trade) — 978-1-9848-5050-8 (ebook) — 978-0-593-40123-1 (digital audio)

DEEP DIVE!

When Ash, Morgan, and three of their fellow Minecraft players, who can actually enter the game, take a deep dive into the Aquatic biome, they find a world filled with beauty and wonder.

978-1-9848-5051-5 (trade) — 978-1-9848-5053-9 (ebook) — 978-0-593-40124-8 (digital audio)

GHAST IN THE MACHINE!

Jodi, Ash, Morgan, and their fellow Minecraft players go out into the real world to find clues to the identity of the mysterious and sinister Evoker King. Not only do they need to find out who—or what—he is, but they need to know if it's really possible for him to escape the game!

978-1-9848-5062-1 (trade) — 978-1-9848-5064-5 (ebook) — 978-0-593-40126-2 (digital audio)

DUNGEON CRAWL!

When Po, Morgan, and three of their fellow Minecraft players track the Evoker King to his home in the heart of a perilous dungeon, they have to gear up for an epic fantasy quest filled with danger, dragons, and hostile mobs.

978-1-9848-5065-2 (trade) — 978-1-9848-5067-6 (ebook) — 978-0-593-40128-6 (digital audio)

LAST BLOCK STANDING!

As the world of Minecraft falls under the Evoker King's control, Morgan, Ash, and their friends get ready for an epic final showdown to save the game they love!

978-1-9848-5069-0 (trade) — 978-1-9848-5071-3 (ebook) — 978-0-593-40130-9 (digital audio)

MINECRAFT
STONESWORD SAGA

CRACK IN THE CODE!

Someone—or something—has turned the Evoker King to stone. And now a new player, Theo, has joined the team on their quest to return their former enemy to normal. But does he have what it takes to be part of the team, or will his meddling put a crack in the game code that none of them will survive?

978-0-593-37298-2 (trade) — 978-0-593-37300-2 (ebook) — 978-0-593-40132-3 (digital audio) — 978-0-593-37299-9 (lib. bdg.)

MOBS RULE!

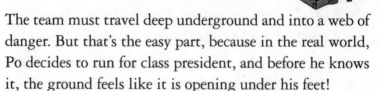

The team must travel deep underground and into a web of danger. But that's the easy part, because in the real world, Po decides to run for class president, and before he knows it, the ground feels like it is opening under his feet!

978-1-9848-5075-1 (trade) — 978-1-9848-5077-5 (ebook) — 978-0-593-50552-6 (digital audio) — 978-1-9848-5076-8 (lib. bdg.)

NEW PETS ON THE BLOCK!

When the third piece of the Evoker King takes the form of a Minecraft witch and sends the team on a quest to bring back an extremely rare animal mob, Jodi is determined to make sure that the mob stays safe!

978-1-9848-5094-2 (trade) — 978-1-9848-5096-6 (ebook) — 978-0-593-55978-9 (digital audio) — 978-1-9848-5095-9 (lib. bdg.)

TOO BEE, OR NOT TO BEE!

The bees around the school and the Stonesword Library are disappearing—and a splinter of the Evoker King has taken on the form of a bee colony with a hive mind! Could there be a connection? And to make matters worse, the rip in the Minecraft sky is growing bigger and darker.

978-0-593-56288-8 (trade) — 978-0-593-56290-1 (ebook) —
978-0-593-66817-7 (digital audio) — 978-0-593-56289-5 (lib. bdg.)

THE GOLEM'S GAME!

The next splinter of the Evoker King takes the form of a golem and challenges each member of the team to run a dangerous obstacle course. Forced to face the challenge alone, the team is not sure they are going to survive the golem's unwinnable game.

978-0-593-56291-8 (trade) — 978-0-593-56293-2 (ebook) —
978-0-593-66817-7 (digital audio) — 978-0-593-56292-5 (lib. bdg.)

THE END OF THE OVERWORLD!

The team has one chance to save Minecraft and their friend the Evoker King—but it may already be too late!

978-0-593-56294-9 (trade) — 978-0-593-56296-3 (ebook) —
978-0-593-79569-9 (digital audio) — 978-0-593-56295-6 (lib. bdg.)

THE ADVENTURES CONTINUE IN

MINECRAFT is a game about placing blocks and going on adventures. Build, play, and explore across infinitely generated worlds of mountains, caverns, oceans, jungles, and deserts. Defeat hordes of zombies, bake the cake of your dreams, venture to new dimensions, or build a skyscraper. What you do in Minecraft is up to you.

Caleb Zane Huett is an author and game designer who lives in Athens, Georgia. His other books include *Top Elf, Buster*, and *Buster Undercover*. When he's not writing, he's almost always playing video and tabletop games. His favorite things in Minecraft are the axolotls.

Alan Batson is a British cartoonist and illustrator. His works include *Everything I Need to Know I Learned from a Star Wars Little Golden Book, Everything That Glitters Is Guy!*, and *Spider-Ham*. Being extremely fond of cubes and travel to exotic places, he has recently begun to lend his talents to several different books on adventures in the world of Minecraft.

Chris Hill is an illustrator living in Birmingham, England, with his wife and two daughters and has been loving it for twenty-five years! When he's not working, he spends time with his family while also trying to tire out his dog on long walks. If there's any time left after that, he loves riding on his motorcycle, feeling the wind on his face while contemplating his next illustration adventure.

JOURNEY INTO THE WORLD OF
MINECRAFT